Princess Navina Visits Mandaat

From the diary of

Count Nef

Drawings by Diana Schuppel Reid

LYTTON PUBLISHING COMPANY
S A N D P O I N T • I D A H O

Direct inquiries to:
Lytton Publishing Co.
335 Lavina Ave.
Sandpoint, Idaho 83864
208-263-3564

Publisher's Note:

Long, long ago, King Hobart Hollenstein, ruler of the Duchy of Pancratica, sent his heir apparent, the Princess Navina, on a world tour to study the governments of other lands. The King believed that the understanding of foreign customs to be gained from such a journey would be the best possible preparation for a future monarch. In command of the touring party was the princess's beloved "Uncle Koko," known to the rest of the court as Baron Kolshic, the King's trusted Minister of Cotillion and Foreign Relations. The histories of the visits are excerpted from the diary of Count Nef, a minor member of the party.

In the adventure previously published, Princess Navina Visits Malvolia, the travellers met the magog of Malvolia. As ruler, he deliberately sought "the greatest misery for the greatest number," as he put it. The princess criticized this philosophy, and as a result, the entire party was put under house arrest. They managed to escape by enlisting the help of a foe of the regime.

According to the Nef diary, the visit to Mandaat was arranged because the baron felt the princess ought to learn about laws, and a correspondent had informed him that "In Mandaat, legislation is the leading industry, and, as a result, they have a plentitude of laws."

"I'm afraid I have very little additional information about the place," said the baron, addressing us on the eve of our arrival in Mandaat. We were seated around the supper table in the aftercabin of the *Giovanni* while Baron Kolshic discussed our upcoming visit.

"All my correspondent says," he continued, smoothing a document on the table before him, "is that Mandaat has, as he puts it, 'a plenitude of laws,' and that before we undertake any action, we should take care to question the natives about its permissibility." The baron looked pointedly at the princess.

She accepted the justice of his implied rebuke. She was quite aware that it had been her boldness that had placed us in such a dangerous situation in Malvolia. "I'll try to be more careful, Uncle Koko," she said. "But," she continued, "sometimes I just can't keep what's inside me, well, inside."

The baron smiled indulgently, for he understood the princess's moods, and the group returned to carbingnac and cheese. I was not easy, however, and suspected that we had not seen the last of complications from the princess's unguarded expression of her "insides."

We had no difficulty berthing our brigantine in the harbor of Mussen, the capital of Mandaat. When we disembarked, we were surprised to find no one about, no welcoming party and no passers-by we could question. The streets were entirely deserted. After pondering this puzzling situation, the baron decided that we should walk to the governmental palace, a gigantic, imposing edifice standing less than two furlongs up the main avenue from the harbor.

No sooner had we begun our stroll when we heard the shrill hooting of a horn, which sounded not unlike the calling of a crow. Following the sound to its source, we saw a short man dressed in a black uniform scurrying down a side street to meet us, blowing this raucous horn all the while. Our first thought was that this individual represented the welcoming party. This was a misjudgement.

"Your mandates please," he said in an abrupt tone.

"I beg your pardon," said the baron.

"Mandates! Show your mandates! What are you waiting for? I am a very busy person!"

"I'm afraid we don't understand," said the baron. "We are voyagers who just . . . ."

"Not again!" said the official, casting his eyes skyward in a gesture of great exasperation. "I spend half my time explaining these regulations to new entrants. It really would be simpler if we just prohibited travellers altogether." He addressed the baron. "To use the streets anywhere in Mandaat, you have to have a mandate. That's all."

"And what, pray, is a mandate?" asked the baron.

"It's a document, a license, that gives you permission to use the streets. It says where you are going *from,* and where you are going *to,* and *when* you are making the trip. No one can be on the streets without one. So get back there." The official poked his club at us in a threatening manner, so that we were forced to retreat back onto the quay.

"But why do you have this law?" asked the princess.

The official regarded her with scorn and impatience.

"Even a fool can see the necessity for it. Why if you didn't regulate the streets, people would go where they wanted when they wanted, and they would bump into each other, and hurt each other. The result would be complete chaos. Mandates keep people from using the same street at the same time."

"But couldn't people avoid hitting each other when they walked on the streets?" persisted the princess. She asked the question politely, but the official grew even more impatient.

"It's obvious you know nothing about human nature, missy! You have no idea how stupid and selfish human beings can be when left free to act on their own. Anyway, I can't waste time discussing it. Wait here until you get your mandates." With that, he turned on his heel and strode away.

Our astonishment at this bizzare custom of Mandaat gave way to a sense of frustration, for we saw we were trapped by a logical imposssibility: we had to have mandates to go somewhere to find out how to get mandates!

Several hours passed as we waited impatiently on the quay. Finally, we spotted a party of officials leave the governmental palace and make their way down the long avenue toward us. This proved to be the welcoming party we had expected.

The leader was a tall, elderly gentleman of distinguished bearing who introduced himself as Dr. Amos Doasdo. He greeted the princess and the baron. "I am so sorry that you had to wait," he said. "We had the greatest difficulty getting our mandates today, otherwise we would have been here in plenty of time to meet you."

"But why do you have these things, these 'mandates,' if they are so inconvenient?" asked the princess.

Dr. Doasdo looked at her with alarm. "Oh, you couldn't do without mandates. They keep society from falling apart. What's a little inconvenience now and then for a system that prevents chaos? Mandates are what we pay for civilization."

"But . . . ." The princess interrupted what she was going to say, having caught a warning look from the baron. Perhaps she had learned some self-discipline from that scrape in Malvolia after all!

Dr. Doasdo had brought mandates for everyone in our party, so we were able to proceed to the

governmental palace. The mandate is a triangular placard which dangles from a chain placed around the neck. It is deliberately large so its presence, or absence, can be detected at a great distance by the commissioners, the officials who enforce the mandate laws. Whatever their benefits to officialdom, mandates are a curse to pedestrians, for they constantly strike against one's knees in a most irritating fashion.

Lodgings had been arranged for us in the Grand Governmental Supreme Palace, as it was called, so that we would have no need of mandates to pass from our sleeping quarters to the offices of government. After a period of rest and unpacking, it was time for the first inspection on our tour, a visit to the legislative body, the Salon die Reglement. Dr. Doasdo had felt that it was most important for us to stop here first. "Here is the heart, and soul, and brain of the country," he said, as he ushered us through the massive door of the visitors' gallery. "This is what makes society function."

We took our seats on the plush red velvet chairs and inspected the strikingly opulent fixtures and finishings of the gigantic chamber. The entire north wall was a mural, intricately done, depicting a burly soldier lifting a rather plump, somewhat muddy maiden from a ditch. The caption below read "Authority Exalts Compassion." The ornaments, statuary, paintings, and gold leaf bespoke fabulous sums spent on decorations. Our expressions of astonishment at the display of grandeur were cut short by a monitor who came down the aisle and insisted on our silence.

We turned to listen to what the orators were saying. The words were incomprehensible.

"Yv xzfgrlfh rm zhhfnrmt blfi mvrtsyli'h rmgvmgrlm gl wl szin," said one.

"Bvh, yvxzfhv gsv yvorvu rm srh vero rmgvmgrlmh droo qfhgrub gsv fhv lu ulixv ztzrmhg srn," said another.

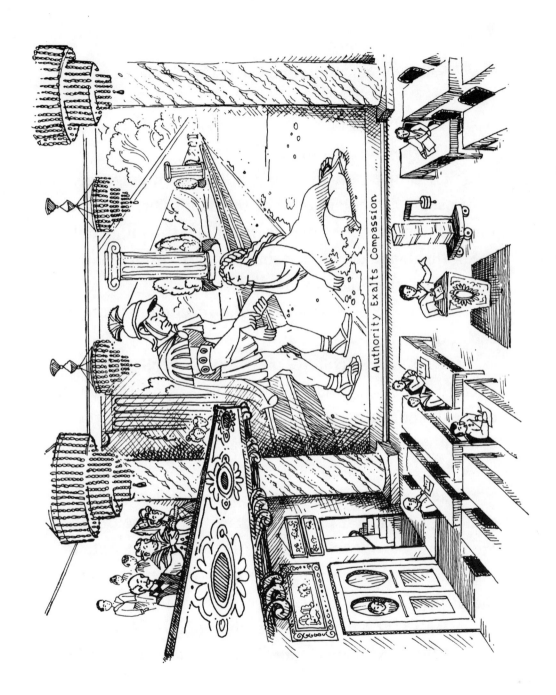

"What language are they speaking?" the baron asked the doctor.

"That is Liberta."

"Do they understand it?"

"Of course not. Liberta is a long-dead language, once used by the aborigines of this land. Out of respect for this minority, we have passed a law forcing people to speak this language on certain formal occasions like meetings of the Salon die Reglement."

"But then, how do the legislators communicate with each other?" asked the baron.

"Well, here, actually, they don't," replied the doctor. "You see, what is said in the Salon is mainly for display. The real work of the body takes place in the committees. That is where the reglamentarians discuss the laws that are voted on."

The doctor then pointed to a tall stack of paper standing on a metal platform. "See, that is the bill they are voting on today. It is the Trifle Regulation Act, number 10,663. We try to have at least three or four of these every year."

"Isn't that a scale it is standing upon?" I asked.

"Why, yes, it is, Count," replied the doctor. "How

clever of you to notice! Yes, we weigh all our legislation here. That is how we evaluate our progress. Last year the Salon approved twenty-nine point three tons of laws, up by nearly a ton over last year. That is how reglamentarians appeal to their constituents, saying how many pounds of laws they proposed, and how many pounds of their proposed laws were approved by the Salon. If the voters think their contributions have been weighty enough, they reelect them."

"Are these gentlemen able to read the laws they are approving?" asked the princess. "Why, that pile alone must be four feet high."

"Of course not," replied the doctor. "No human being could read so much."

"But shouldn't they understand the laws they are approving?"

"My dear, that would never do. If they waited until they knew what they were voting on, they would never get anything done."

At that moment, the monitor returned and scolded us for talking. The doctor decided it would be best to exit and continue the conversation in the hall.

Once the gallery door had closed behind us, the

princess spoke. "But surely it's silly for people to pass laws they don't know anything about. When I become Queen of Pancratica I'm going to read all the laws I approve."

The doctor seemed somewhat offended by her remark, but he maintained a civil, if stern, tone in replying. "You fail to understand, madam, the real purpose of legislation."

"Isn't it to make things better?" asked the princess.

"Ha! That is precisely where your thinking goes astray. The passage of laws has almost nothing to do with making things better. The real purpose of legislation is reassurance." The doctor had regained his genial tone as he moved onto obviously familiar ground.

"You see, human beings are a naturally frightened species, afraid of things outside their understanding and control. They need to believe in some power capable of knowing about and commanding these worrisome objects. In some societies, they have what are called 'witch doctors,' who wave sticks and colored flags at the sun. Here in Mandaat, our reglementarians perform this function. They reassure the populace that they are in control of strange and menacing phenomena. The key to this role is being energetic, busy. After all, what would people think of a witch doctor who waved a stick at the sun only once a year? So you see, that is why the passage of a large volume of laws is so important, and why the reglementarians don't need to understand their content."

There was an awkward silence after this statement by Doctor Doasdo. Since he had spoken with such authority, no one cared to question him further. The doctor's official post, as he had explained to us during our introductions that morning, was that of Justificator. It was his duty to explain to visitors and critics, concerning every aspect of the regime of Mandaat, that whatever is, is right.

It being lunchtime, we were conducted along the corridors of the Supreme Palace to one of the many dining rooms located in the building. This room was decorated in the same lavish style as all other parts of the Palace. Whoever suffered in Mandaat, it was not officials of the regime.

When we were seated, the waiters brought our plates, already served, containing a meat prepared a la Chateau D'if, and a puree of potatoes. After all were served, and no one began to eat, the princess took up her fork, assuming that it was her role to commence.

The doctor rested his hand on her elbow. "I'm afraid we must wait, Princess." The princess put down her fork, blushing in embarrassment.

Several minutes passed. Finally, the princess asked, "What are we waiting for?"

"For the meat and potatoes to be inspected," replied the doctor. "It is one of our laws that no one may eat meat or potatoes in any restaurant unless it is approved by a government inspector after it has been served."

The doctor turned to the rest of the party. "You may, however, eat bread and drink water. These do not need inspection." He dropped his voice and added, "Yet." He took up a roll and beckoned to the others to do likewise. "Feel free," he said. "Feel free." We noticed then that all those at the tables around us were eating only bread and drinking only water, while their plates of meat and potatoes were untouched.

"What is the point of this inspection law?" asked the princess.

"Why, of course, it's to keep the restaurant from serving tainted or poisonous food," replied the doctor.

"But can't you depend on the cooks and waiters not to serve food if it is bad?"

"Oh, dear no. You have no idea how stupid and selfish human beings can be when left free to act on their own," replied the doctor.

"Has this inspection system greatly reduced the number of cases of illness due to tainted food?" The baron asked the question as a way of giving Dr. Doasdo an opportunity to expound the virtues of the arrangement. He did not get the answer he expected.

"No, not at all," the doctor replied. "The number of cases of restaurant food poisoning continues the same as before the law was adopted."

"But then that makes the law doubly silly," exclaimed the princess. "Doesn't it?"

"My dear, you have forgotton the point I was just making in the hall." The sternness had crept into the doctor's tone again. "About reassurance."

The princess looked puzzled at first, and then brightened. "Oh, I see. You mean that people are reassured by the idea that the government is inspecting the food, whether it makes any difference or not?"

"Precisely!" said the doctor, pleased with the success of his instruction.

We waited about twenty more minutes, tasting the bread and sipping water. Then an elderly official entered from the kitchen door. "Ah, there's the meat inspector now," said Dr. Doasdo.

The inspector came to our table and tore off tickets from his pad, and placed one beside each plate. Each ticket declared, in rather lengthy language, that the meat had been inspected and declared safe. We noticed that he did not appear to look at the meat at all.

"Now we may begin," said the doctor, "on the meat, that is."

"You mean, there's another inspector for the potatoes?" asked the princess in disbelief. The doctor nodded quietly.

Thereupon, Count Zinn, a minor member of our party, entered the conversation. The count tries to impress others by making what he fancies are intelligent observations. "Couldn't this inefficiency be easily rectified, Dr. Doasdo? Why could not legislation be drafted that specified that the meat *and* potatoes be inspected together, by the same person?"

"An excellent suggestion, Count," said the doctor. "And so much in keeping with the spirit of our civilization here in Mandaat! We believe in the continual revision of our laws. Among other things, it means that opposition to them never has a chance to build. I shall put you in touch with a reglamentarian I know well, Professor Gowidt D'fleau. You can explain your idea to him, so that he may propose it to the Salon in the form of a law."

We began to eat our meat, which, being stone cold, was of course far from appetizing. We noticed that at the other tables the diners left their seats as soon as they had finished their meat, leaving their potatoes untouched. The doctor suggested we do the same. "I believe the potato inspector is not due to arrive for some time yet," he said in an apologetic tone.

"Oh dear," said the princess. "If this happens every day, I guess we just won't eat potatoes in Mandaat."

Count Zinn interposed, "Don't worry, Princess. Wait for the passage of the Zinn Act!" The count was rather full of himself.

We Visit a Church and a School

We passed the early part of the afternoon in our rooms, getting accustomed to our living arrangements. We discovered that in each room there was a large bundle of documents. After some preliminaries, I had just settled into reading these materials when I heard a loud thump coming from the princess's chamber. I rushed down the hall as the baron himself was opening her door.

"What is the matter?" he asked.

The princess was apparently in a provoked mood and chose not to reply. One of her maids-in-waiting answered the baron.

"She bumped the papers onto the floor, sir, accidentally-like."

The stack of documents had been strewn across the floor of the room. "It appears to have been a rather energetic accident," said the baron dryly.

"Silly!" said the princess. "Silly, silly, silly, silly! All these permits. Permits to turn on the water, permits to turn off the water, permits to open the door, permits to close the door. Why there's even a permit to pick up coins off the floor, if they should happen to fall!''

"Now Navi," said the baron gently, "I'm sure there's a good reason behind them.''

"But Uncle Koko, nobody *knows* if we are doing these things. Watch!" She went over to the sink and turned the water tap on and off several times. "See: who can know if I did it?" She scuffed at the papers with her foot, and then sat down on a footstool. She thought a moment and then said, "Reassurance. That is what Dr. Doasdo would say is what all these permits are for. But Uncle Koko, I wonder, what is wrong with the Mandaatians that they should need *so much* reassurance?''

"Perhaps you have a point, Navi," the baron replied, "but still, we had better have the maids pick these permits up and pile them neatly. Since the Mandaatians *are* so insecure, they are likely to be very touchy about anyone who disrespects their customs.''

Later that afternoon, Dr. Doasdo called for us to take us on a tour of a local church. While we were riding in the carriage (we had again been supplied with mandates), the baron questioned the doctor about the church administration. We had been given to understand

that the church was a compulsory governmental body, and the baron began the conversation on this point.

"Tell me, Doctor, there are some who say that attendance at religious services ought not to be compulsory, that it ought to be a matter of individual choice and conscience. How do you answer that view?"

"Here in Mandaat, we believe religion is too important to be left to choice. Churches provide the training that enables our people to be responsible citizens. It can't be left to opinion or chance whether some people will get this training or not. They would end up being deprived of essential tools of successful modern living."

"I see," said the baron. "But could not religion be supported by voluntary donations?"

"My dear Baron," replied the doctor, "if we did not force people to pay for religion through taxes, we could never support the huge cost of our religious establishment."

"But could you not rely on usage fees, charging each person for attending?"

The doctor was beginning to grow irritated. "Surely, Baron, as a statesman yourself, you should realize the inequity of such an idea. What would happen to the poor? They could not afford to pay the attendance fees, and would be left without religious instruction. No, the only fair way is universal compulsory religion.''

The baron, seeing that the doctor was becoming upset, asked no more questions and we rode in silence the rest of the way.

The church building was a drab structure with a sign identifying it only as ''C. S. 104.'' We noticed that several windows were broken and slogans—some quite vulgar—had been painted on the walls. We were introduced to the superintendent, a slight, nervous man who continually held his hands clenched together.

The princess began the interview pointing to the slogans which were painted on the walls. ''Why do you do this?'' she asked.

''Oh, dear, dear, *we* don't do it. It is done by some of the parishioners who misbehave. They also break the windows, and sometimes even set fires. It's very sad.''

''But why do they misbehave?''

''We don't really know. It has deep, complex social causes that are rooted in the failings of society. It certainly isn't their fault. All we can hope to do here is cope.''

"Why don't you expel them?" asked the princess.

"Oh dear, dear, you can't do that. Everybody is entitled to religion in Mandaat. And besides, we are forcing them to come. Church truancy is a serious crime in Mandaat. Heavens, being expelled is probably just what they would want. No, coping—and, of course, more funding—that is the only way to handle the situation." The superintendent turned to the baron, "Would you like to see a service?"

He led us down the hall and opened the door of a rather large room. The din was enormous. There were several hundred people inside. Most were conversing with each other, all talking at once, some were eating, and throwing litter on the floor, a few were reading newspapers, and several were stretched on the floor, apparently sleeping. The administrator drew our attention to a woman standing on a platform at the end of the room. Shouting to make himself heard over the noise, he said, "She's reading the sermon."

He closed the door again. "We have copies of that sermon, just in case people don't get to hear it. I'll bring you one." He went down the hall and returned with a document which he handed to the baron.

"At least it talks about God," said the baron, but his face grew troubled as he looked at it more carefully. "Very interesting," he said in that careful tone he has when something is amiss. The document was passed around and we saw what had disturbed the baron. The word "God" was there, but no words with any meaning.

For example, the first sentence read:

— the — God — the — and the —.

"What does it mean?" asked the princess. "Where are all the other words?"

"They have been edited out," replied the superintendent. "You see, Princess, our sermons are written by the Board of Sermons, which is under the control of the Salon die Reglement, which speaks, of course, for all the people of Mandaat. Therefore, nothing can be in a sermon which does not meet the approval of all the people. After all, since everyone is being forced to fund religion, that's only fair.

"When religion was nationalized, back in the third epoch, they began with the religious materials they had at the time, and gradually the Sermons Board eliminated the points objected to by this or that group. For example, that first sentence originally said 'In the beginning God created the heavens and the earth.' Well, there were some who disputed that God created the heavens, and others who argued that He did not create the earth, and others who thought God came after the beginning of time. As a result of these objections, the passage was edited. In this way," the superintendent said proudly, "we have at last got sermons that serve the needs of the entire community."

There was a long, strained silence. Count Zinn, always eager to put himself forward, spoke. "But is this religion? I mean, what's left, is it correct to call it religion?"

"That's a highly metaphysical question, sir," replied the superintendent. "All I can say is that the government of Mandaat appropriated twelve hundred and sixty-two trillion mandoliers last year for 'religion' and, by jum, that's a good enough definition for me!"

There being nothing more to be shown at the church, we exchanged pleasantries and took our leave. Although we were careful not to say anything in the presence of Dr. Doasdo, it was clear that all members of our party were rather shocked at what had become of religion in Mandaat.

On the route back to the Supreme Palace, the princess spotted a handsome building. "That is one of our schools, Princess," said the doctor. "Apparently it emphasizes mathematics." the sign on the lawn in front said "Solomon Wise School of Mathematical Excellence."

"Can we stop and see it?" asked the princess.

The doctor seemed uneasy. "Strictly speaking, stopping here is not covered in our mandate." He paused a moment. "Let's do this: while you go in to see the school, I will remain here in the carriage, and can say we haven't really stopped, but have only paused to lubricate the axles. But don't take too long!"

We left the carriage and, our mandates clanking about our knees, walked to the building. At the entrance, we were met by the master, as the director of the school was called. He seemed quite eager to explain the school to us. "We emphasize mathematics here, since mathematics is what will save the world: exact thinking, accurate thinking, honest thinking. So we are rather strict and demanding. Every child masters algebra by age 10, spherical geometry by age 11, and can use, *and derive from first principles* the differential calculus by age 12!"

"That certainly seems wonderful," said the baron. "But what about the classics? Don't you feel these are important in the education of the young?"

"We teach a little classics, sir, but frankly it's merely an introduction. We can't devote that much time to it if we are to give a thorough grounding in mathematics. Furthermore, classics instructors won't get along with our mathematicians. They want dress codes, for example—which we abhor—and would want to make many other changes. If we included first-rate classics teachers in our faculty, the result would be many compromises and a watering-down of the curriculum for everyone. And besides, if parents want their children to have classics, there are plenty of schools specializing in that, and some of them do marvels.''

''What about the point that since everyone is being forced to fund education through the tax system, what is offered in the school should be acceptable to everyone?''

The master raised his eyebrows. ''You must indeed be new to this country,'' he said. ''Here in Mandaat, government has nothing to do with education. It's in our constitution: separation of school and state. All our money is raised privately, mainly from attendance fees. Therefore, we may specialize in whatever beliefs, subjects, and theories we think are valid.''

''That is a surprise,'' said the baron. ''But what happens to the poor? If they cannot afford to pay the attendance fees, are they not left without any educational instruction whatsoever?''

''Ah, sir, money is never the problem. You see, we *believe* in what we do. We want as many qualified children to have mathematical training as possible. If a child comes to us, capable of receiving our training, it pains us to turn that child away. So we devise ways to fund students that cannot afford our training. We set the fees of the other students higher to cover these children;

we get them special jobs so they can work to pay part of their fees; and we have a scholarship fund to which graduates and philanthropists contribute.''

"This may work here," replied the baron, "but I doubt it could apply in my country. In our duchy, we could not do without state funding of schools.''

"Do you really think so? Tell me, sir, do you have state funding of religion in your country?''

"Of course not," declared the baron energetically, the vision of state-funded religion fresh in his mind.

"Does it happen, then, that people are turned away from your churches owing to an inability to pay? Are they excluded from services, or teachings, or listening to the music, on account of their poverty?''

"No," replied the baron. "I see your point. Somehow, other contributors make up the difference.''

"And that is exactly what happens here with our schools," the master concluded. "Would you like to see a class in action?''

He led us down the hall and opened a door. Inside we could see about twenty boys and girls listening to a teacher in the front of the room. She was speaking about something mathematical that I only partly understood, about "signs" and, I believe, "tangerines." Some of the children, hearing us in the hall, turned to look at us, but the teacher immediately regained their attention saying, "Eyes front, please."

When the master had closed the door, the princess said, "They seem wonderfully well behaved. And they don't seem to write on the walls either," she added, pointing to the walls of the neatly-kept corridor.

"Oh, we insist on discipline here," replied the master. "Without discipline, you cannot teach mathematics, and if you cannot teach mathematics, you cannot save the world. It's that simple!" His eyes gleamed with enthusiasm.

"And besides, everyone here wants to be here. Why shouldn't they listen carefully to their teachers?"

As we returned down the hall, the baron spoke. "On this question of voluntary schooling, what do you say to the argument that education is too important to be left to choice or accident? Don't schools provide the training that enables people to be responsible citizens? Shouldn't everyone be required to go to school?"

"What a horrible thought, forcing people to go to school!" The master shuddered. "We have a very high opinion of education. We see it as valuable, even precious, not something repugnant, like a medicine that people must be forced to take. Why, imagine what this school would turn into if our students were driven here by soldiers and policemen! It would be almost as bad as a church!''

We thanked the master for his explanations and excused ourselves, citing the problem with the mandates as the cause of our hasty departure.

''I understand,'' said the master, with a sympathetic glance at the placards dangling at our knees. ''After all, mandates are what we pay for civilization.'' His right eye seemed to wink at that moment, which made it uncertain if he was sincere in saying this.

Once in the carriage, the baron commented, ''I find it somewhat surprising that here in Mandaat the government does not control education.''

''But Baron,'' replied the doctor, ''this is a part of our constitution: separation of school and state. Mandaat is a free country, after all!''

There was silence for a time as the horses went clip-clopping down the avenue. Then the doctor spoke again.

"Of course, I agree that private education, being unregulated, is open to many abuses. It is not very reassuring to think that in education, people may do anything they like." He paused, staring thoughtfully out the window. "Not reassuring at all."

The Princess Goes Underground!

It was perhaps too much to expect the princess to remain clear of trouble for the entire visit. She has royal blood, and royal blood has a way of provoking complications in even the most innocent situations. Certainly no crisis had a more innocent beginning than what happened to the princess in Mandaat.

Our rooms in the Supreme Palace were on the first floor on the east side. They faced, across a rather narrow street, a block of tenement houses where some Mandaatian families lived. On the afternoon after our visit to the church and school, the princess was sitting at the window of her room, idly watching the houses across the way. She was exceedingly bored, for nothing was planned on our tour, and of course she could not go out on the streets because of the mandate regulations.

Gazing upon the houses opposite, the princess spotted a child, a three- or four-year-old girl, sitting in an open window, playing with a doll. She waved at this child, who smiled with delight and began to wave back in a most vigorous fashion. In the act of waving, however, the child let the doll slip, and it tumbled down to the street!

The princess scarcely hesitated. She saw the child was beginning to cry over losing the doll, a loss which the princess herself had, indirectly, caused. She ran down to the street door. Glancing up and down the street, she saw no sign of commissioners, and assumed that she could cross without detection. She rushed across the street, retrieved the doll and handed it back to the child in the window.

At just that moment, she heard a shrill, crow-like honking. Alas, a commissioner had been lurking in a doorway at the far end of the street! "Caw! caw! caw!" went his horn as he rushed up the street toward the princess. Perhaps this noise frightened the princess, or perhaps she had reached some kind of breaking point with all the restrictions of Mandaat. Whatever the reason, she was unwilling to allow the officer to apprehend her. Instead, she turned and fled down the street!

In response, the commissioner's horn changed pitch to a shriller, louder note. Apparently, this was a signal to other commissioners in the vicinity to join the chase after a mandate-evader. Almost immediately, the princess was being pursued by an entire band of little commissioners, in their little black suits, all honking their little horns, like a flock of angry crows chasing a sparrow.

The noise terrified the princess, who ran faster and faster, down the street, then around the corner, then up another street and around another corner. This burst of speed got her ahead of the commissioners for a moment. Unfortunately, her shipboard life had left her in an unexercized condition, and she had to stop for lack of breath. The shrill caw-cawing began to draw closer, but she could hardly move her feet. Then she heard a sound from a doorway.

"Psst! Psst!" A young man was waving at her to enter. She had little choice if she was to escape her pursuers. She stepped inside and the young man quickly closed the door behind her.

"Oh, thank you!" she said, haltingly gasping out each word.

"My pleasure," he replied. "Come upstairs."

He led the princess up two long flights of stairs—she had to pause several times to catch her breath—to a small third-story room where a number of boys were seated on the floor. He invited her to sit on the floor, and then called out, "Cora! We have another evader! Bring something for her to drink!"

Then he turned to the princess. "This," he said, indicating the group, "is the Amac-Amic Underground Group." The boys smiled at her in welcome. "We are one of hundreds of such underground societies, of people who challenge the mandate laws and act to assist others, like yourself, who are being pursued by the commissioners. We believe that the mandate laws, like all the laws of Mandaat, are immoral. It is our goal to undermine this regime!"

"I certainly want to thank you for saving me from those men," replied the princess. "And I agree that the mandate laws seem most silly and unfair, as are just about all the other laws here that I've seen."

At that moment, an old woman hobbled into the

room carrying a steaming mug. She had a warm, kindly face and welcomed the princess with a broad smile. "This is Cora," said the young man, "and my name is Rebbie."

The princess took the mug and tasted the drink, which was called "lotz." It was not unlike hot cider, except that it had a stronger taste and, as the princess was to discover, a stronger effect!

Sipping her drink, surrounded by the friendly boys, the princess felt safe and content. They asked her many questions about Pancratica which she was pleased to answer. Then she asked them about their group and its purposes. She learned that its name was taken from that of an early chief of the Liberta tribe.

"When are you planning to start your revolution, Rebbie?" asked the princess.

"Why never," he replied. "You see, we don't believe in revolution."

"That is a surprise. I thought all revolutionaries believe in revolution."

"Ah, but we're not revolutionaries. We don't believe in trying to knock over the regime by force. As history shows, all that brings is the new use of force by the

revolutionaires once they are victorious. They set up a new government which makes more laws enforced by more policemen and commissioners, and pretty soon you're back to where you started.

"No, Princess, we are not revolutionaries. We are nibblelaries! We nibble at the laws, so as to make them harder and harder to enforce. We evade them, just enough not to get caught, or we stretch them to confound their original intent. That is how we challenge the mandate laws. We dart across streets, and then run away, too quickly for the commissioners to be able to catch us. As more and more people join us, the laws will simply become unenforceable!

"I see," said the princess. "And when this regime is overthrown—"

"Undermined," corrected Rebbie.

"—Undermined, I mean, what will you replace it with?"

"Nothing!" responded Rebbie. "No rules, no regulations, no laws, no anything. Then everybody will be able to do as they please."

"But won't there be chaos?"

Rebbie smiled and a few of the boys giggled. "I see

you've been listening to the reglamentarians' propaganda.'' He paused to choose his words. ''What's chaos? What do you mean by 'chaos'?''

The princess thought a moment. ''Does it mean people dying?''

''But people die in Mandaat every day,'' replied Rebbie. ''The Salon die Reglement doesn't stop that.''

''Maybe it means people bumping into each other?'' ventured the princess.

Rebbie smiled, ''Do you realize that as a result of the mandate laws, we have built tunnels and corridors under the city so people can get around. They are full of people walking back and forth. The Salon doesn't do a thing about it, because they know if they regulated halls and tunnels, we'd all starve!''

''Then maybe chaos means people being unhappy?'' asked the princess.

''And the Salon has prevented unhappiness in Mandaat?'' asked Rebbie, throwing his arms apart. The boys smiled at his theatrics.

''No,'' he continued, '''chaos' has nothing to do with the actual daily lives of Mandaatians. It refers to the illusion of control. Each person in the government seeks to force others to do his will. That's what a person means when he speaks of 'chaos.' He means that people are not doing what *he* wants them to do.''

The princess suddenly realized she was becoming extremely sleepy. Something about the lotz was making her mind slip. There was another question she wanted to ask Rebbie, but she could not seem to pull it from her brain. ''But what about...?'' That was all she said before she fell into a deep, quiet slumber.

While the princess had gone to ground in Rebbie's hiding place, at the palace the baron had to grapple with the difficulty caused by her disappearance. Of course, the maids had seen her flight from the commissioners. The baron decided that to avoid scandal and possibly something worse, it was best to keep her law-breaking from the authorities.

At supper that evening, Dr. Doasdo inquired about her. The baron declared her to be sick, but he failed to reckon with the thoroughness of this highly regulated society.

''I'm afraid, then, that she must have a sickness permit,'' said the doctor.

''Indeed?'' queried the baron.

"Yes, she must be inspected by a physician, for she might have something contagious, you see."

"My, my," said the baron, "you do indeed have many regulations here in Mandaat!"

"Yes, Baron, and notice how they reinforce each other. It's like a giant spider web. Each regulation gives us an opportunity to detect law-breaking of another kind. Of course, that wouldn't apply in this case."

"No, of course not," replied the baron.

The physician-inspector arrived at our quarters later that evening, and it seemed inevitable that the princess's absence would then be discovered. But the baron surprised us with his strategem!

He first told the physician that he could not be allowed to see the princess because the laws of Pancratica forbade the princess to be thus immodestly exposed.

The physician granted the point—he was most sympathetic when it came to legal requirements—but continued to insist that he could not give a permit without seeing the princess.

"Tell me, Doctor," asked the baron, "must you see *all* of the princess? Surely you don't inspect every square inch, even the soles of the feet, and so on?" The physician admitted it was true, that he did not need to see all of a patient to give a permit.

"Then I believe we can arrange a compromise," said the baron. He led the physician to the princess's boudoir. He rapped upon the door, "Princess, we are ready for the examination."

The door opened just a crack, and a delicate, feminine hand was extended (the hand, of course, of one of the maids). "Here, Doctor," said the baron grandly, "is the part of the princess you are duly authorized to examine!"

The medical man accepted this declaration, made his examination of the hand, signed the permit and left! In this way, we were able to keep news of the princess's disappearance from the officials of Mandaat.

Meanwhile, in Rebbie's hideout, the princess was having a long sleep. When she awoke, the sun was streaming in through the windows and the room was empty. She found that a blanket had been put over her. "Hello?" she called out.

Cora came from the adjoining room. "Good morning, dearie. Good afternoon, that is, for you've slept nearly a day!"

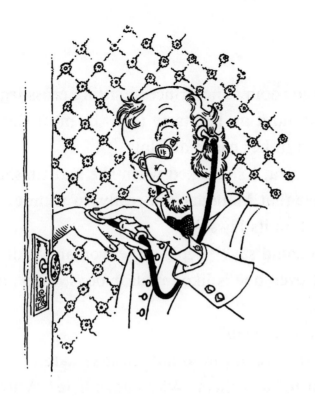

"It must have been the lotz," said the princess. "It was stronger than I thought." Then she remembered her position. "Oh my goodness, I must get back to the palace! What shall I do?"

"Don't worry about a thing," said Cora patiently. "Rebbie and the boys will fix it. They know how to do such things. But first let me get you a nice breakfast, for you must be famished!"

Cora brought a breakfast, which had to be spread out on the floor, as there were no tables—or any other furniture—in the room. The princess, sitting cross-legged on the floor, found it no less tasty than the most elegant feast ever served in her castle at Plotz.

"Tell me, Cora," she asked when she had finished, "Do you believe that Mandaat can really do without its government and all its laws?"

"Ay, who could say?" replied the woman. "All I know is that if everyone is like my dear boys, then no, it never could work."

"What do you mean?"

"Because they're not even able to take care of themselves, not to say others. Who cooks here? Who picks up here? You should have seen this room after they left last night: paper, food, mugs all over. I pick it all up. Don't take me wrong. I love my boys like sons, and I don't mind doin' for 'em." She collected the breakfast things and removed them to the kitchen.

When she returned, she said, "Oh, they're good at sneaking around, and foiling the commissioners. But I say, how are the streets going to be clean? The streets are clean now, because the government does it. When there's no government and just my boys running up and down, do you think the streets are going to be clean?"

"I think I see what you mean," said the princess.

Shortly afterwards, Rebbie entered with two of the boys. "Ah, Sleeping Beauty is awake," he said with mock grandness, "and desires to be wafted back to her castle." The princess giggled. She thanked Cora and took her leave.

She followed Rebbie down the stairs and into the basement. There he led the party into a small, low tunnel that had been roughly hacked out of the earth. Soon, this tunnel connected to a larger passage that was full of people walking rapidly back and forth. "See, Princess, this is how we Mandaatians get around."

"They don't seem to be bumping into each other, particularly," said the princess.

Rebbie gave a conspiratorial wink. He led her along the main corridor for several blocks and then turned up a flight of stairs. "Here we must cross the street, for the tunnel does not run in this direction. We will wait for the decoys to clear the way." The boys went out first. Their assignment was to draw the commissioners away, by running down the street in opposite directions. The sound of caw-cawing soon reached their ears.

"Quick!" said Rebbie. "Across the street!"

They dashed across the street, down a stairway and into another tunnel, where they joined a crowd of people. Passing along the corridor for several more blocks, they came to a door. "This is the stairway up to the palace, Princess. Here is where I say goodby."

There was an awkward moment as they looked into each other's eyes. Then the princess gave Rebbie a quick hug, turned and entered the door.

She quietly shut it behind her. Before her was a highly ornamented spiral staircase made of iron. Gathering the folds of her dress with one hand, she began to tiptoe up the steps. She had gone about halfway when the door at the top opened and an official came clanking down the stairs in his big leather boots. The princess, unsure of her position, turned around and began descending. The official spotted her.

"Stop there!" he said as he came rushing down the stairs. "What do you think you are doing?"

Though he was eager to catch her in the wrong, he obviously did not yet know what transgression the princess had committed. She saw a chance to trick him. "I was intending to leave the palace," she said.

"Do you have a palace-leaving permit?" he asked.

"Well, no, not exactly," she replied.

"Then you cannot leave," he said sternly. "You must go back and get a palace-leaving permit—and of course a palace-returning permit to be able to come back in."

"I'm terribly sorry," said the princess. With a nice display of reluctance in her step, she climbed the stairs, while the official glared at her from below, to see that she followed his order.

She went through the door at the top, breathless and triumphant, and found herself in one of the corridors of the palace. Adopting a firm, authoritative manner, so that no official might challenge her, she walked briskly along the passages—making a few wrong turnings in the process—until she at last arrived at the door of her chambers.

She was greeted with great joy by her maids-in-waiting. The baron was, of course, relieved and delighted at her safe return, though he made a show of scolding her for her impetuous behavior. The princess bubbled with high spirits as she recounted her adventures. I fear she was rather exhilarated at having successfully defied the bureaucracy of Mandaat. She even claimed to be "a little bit of a nibblelary."

There is little more to tell of our visit to Mandaat, for we left the afternoon following the princess's return. However, an episode of note occurred at the final luncheon at the Supreme Palace. We had been served our meat and potatoes and were waiting, as usual, for the meat inspector. When this gentleman finally appeared, he surprised us by not coming to the tables. Instead, he took a position by the wall.

"Why aren't you inspecting the meat?" Dr. Doasdo called to him.

The man came over to our table. "Because, as of today, new regulations have relieved me of this job. The nincompoops up above"—he jerked his thumb in the direction of the Salon die Reglement—"have decided that the potato inspector is also given the duty of inspecting the meat. Since that inspector is inspecting the sawdust at the mill, he won't be here for several hours.

"That's why nothing ever works in Mandaat," he went on, "because they have idiots making the laws. If they would just get intelligent, sincere people as reglementarians, they could fix all these problems."

We then remembered the proposal to improve the inspections. Everyone looked at Count Zinn, who made himself small and stared intently into the water glass he held between his hands. Our meal that day consisted of bread and water only.

* * *

Several days later, at supper on the *Giovanni,* we were discussing the government of Mandaat and trying to explain how it grew into its present oppressive form.

"What puzzles me," said the Baron, "is that the regime is quite without any theory or guiding ideology. Each measure is approved simply out of a desire to improve things, or to reassure the public"—the baron smiled at the princess. "Yet the result is a state more dictatorial than one governed by religious zealots."

I added. "If Mandaat has any official ideology it is probably the philosophy of freedom of the Liberta natives, a philosophy wholly transgressed in practice even while lip service is paid to it."

"Perhaps," said Count Zinn, "The real problem is that Mandaat does not have enough sincere public officials."

The Princess was on him immediately. "How can you be so silly, Count? The idea of having a single inspector at the restaurant was your idea, and you were sincere. Yet that left us without any lunch at all!" The count bowed his head in embarrassment. "No," she continued, "it's not the sincerity of the reglamentarians. The problem with Mandaat is that it has too many laws, too many for anyone to manage properly."

She turned to the baron, "How many laws is the right number for a country to have?"

"Mandaat did indeed have too many," he replied.

"But if reducing the number of laws makes a country better, couldn't you keep going? I mean, make the country better and better by having fewer and fewer laws? Until you'd end up with no laws at all!"

"How silly you are, Navi," replied the baron. "You have to have laws. Otherwise there'd be no point in having a government."

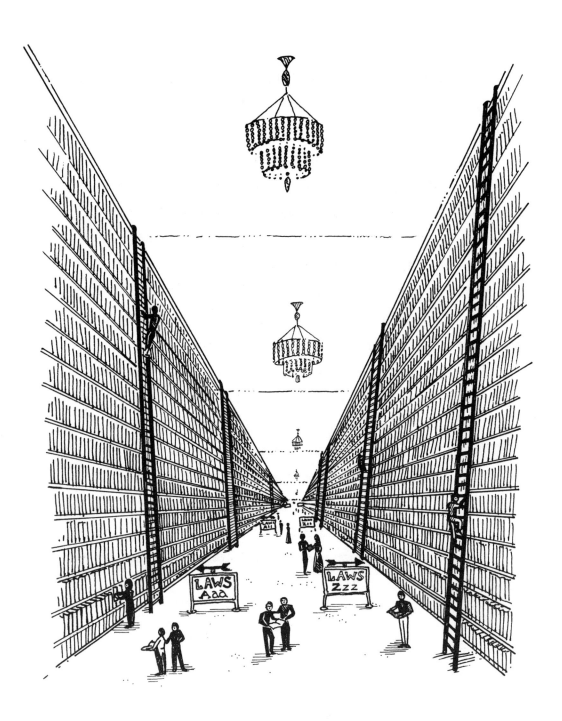

"But do you have to have a government? Rebbie doesn't think you have to have a government."

"Accept what I'm saying, Navi, that's all toffle-boffle. It's inconceivable to have a country without a government."

At that point in our travels, we had no grounds for questioning the baron's declaration.